THE AWFUL MESS

By Anne Rockwell

Four Winds Press
New York

Library of Congress Cataloging in Publication Data

Rockwell, Anne F
The awful mess.

Reprint of the ed. published by Parents' Magazine Press, New York.

Summary: Though his family only sees an awful mess, Olly knows his room contains a cave with wild animals, a traffic jam, and a tunnel to crawl through.

[1. Cleanliness—Fiction] I. Title.
[PZ7.R5943Aw 1980]   [E]   80-16779
ISBN 0-590-07784-8

Published by Four Winds Press
A division of Scholastic Magazines, Inc., New York, N.Y.
Copyright © 1973 by Anne Rockwell
All rights reserved
Printed in the United States of America
Library of Congress Catalog Card Number: 80-16779
1 2 3 4 5 84 83 82 81 80

For Hannah,
Elizabeth and Oliver

In Olly's room there was a tunnel

and two tall towers

and a bad traffic jam.

Wild animals lived in a deep,
dark cave.

The big kids said,

"Your room

is an awful mess!"

His mother said,
"Olly, please put away your toys."
"Uh-uh," said Olly.

His father said,
"Olly, please put your toys away."

But Olly wouldn't.

He started building a third tower instead.

And his mother and father said,
"Well, after all, it's *his* room."

The big kids said,
"It sure is an awful mess!"

Next day Olly's mother went away.

His baby-sitter said,
"My goodness. What an awful mess!"

And she turned the towers
into neat rows of blocks.

The traffic jam went into the toy chest.

The wild animals came
out of the deep, dark cave

and went to bed.

After the baby-sitter had gone home
Olly shut his door and worked

and worked.

"Oh my," said his mother.

"Hmmmm," said his father.

"Wow! What a mess," said his brother and sister.

"It's *my* room!" shouted Olly, and
went to bed.

Next day it rained.
His mother had company
who had a boy named David.

They went up to play in Olly's room.

And they crawled through the tunnel,
past the jungle,
past the traffic jam and the towers

and the big engine that turned.
Olly's flashlight lit the way.

When they got to the end of the tunnel
they ate the two caramels that David
had in his pocket.

And David said, "I *like* your room.
It's neat!"